Henny

To the memory of Edith Dunbar,

gatekeeper of my childhood

SIMON & SCHUSTER BOOKS FOR YOUNG READERS

An imprint of Simon & Schuster Children's Publishing Division

1230 Avenue of the Americas, New York, New York 10020

Copyright © 2014 by Elizabeth Rose Stanton

For information about special discounts for bulk purchases, please contact Simon & Schuster Special Sales at 1-866-506-1949 or business@simonandschuster.com.

The Simon & Schuster Speakers Bureau can bring authors to your live event. For more information or to book an event,

contact the Simon & Schuster Speakers Bureau at 1-866-248-3049 or visit our website at www.simonspeakers.com.

Book design by Lucy Ruth Cummins

The text for this book is set in Myster.

The illustrations for this book are rendered in pencil and watercolor.

Manufactured in China / 1013 SCP

2 4 6 8 10 9 7 5 3 1

Library of Congress Cataloging-in-Publication Data

Stanton, Elizabeth Rose, author, illustrator.

Henny / Elizabeth Rose Stanton. — First edition.

pages cm

"A Paula Wiseman Book."

Summary: "Henny, a chick with arms, discovers the benefits of being different."— Provided by publisher.

ISBN 978-1-4424-8436-8 (hardcover : alk. paper) — ISBN 978-1-4424-8438-2 (eBook)

1. Chickens—Fiction. 2. Individuality—Fiction. 3. Self-acceptance—Fiction. 4. Humorous stories.   I. Title.

PZ7.S79326He 2014

E —dc23

2012047858

Henny

Elizabeth Rose Stanton

A PAULA WISEMAN BOOK · SIMON & SCHUSTER BOOKS FOR YOUNG READERS

New York London Toronto Sydney New Delhi

Henny was not a *typical chicken.*

Henny was born with arms.

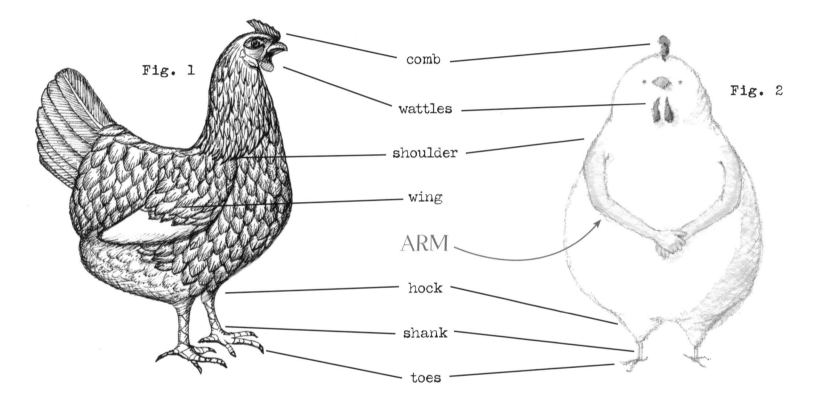

Fig. 1

comb

wattles

shoulder

wing

ARM

hock

shank

toes

TYPICAL CHICKEN

Fig. 2

Henny

Henny's mother was very surprised,

but she loved Henny anyway.

Sometimes Henny liked having arms
and sometimes she didn't.

She liked it when they fluttered
behind her like ribbons when she ran.

She didn't like it when she
always had to go last.

She liked being different.

She *didn't* like being different.

As Henny grew, her worries grew too.

She worried about being

right-handed

or left-handed.

She worried about what to wear. . . .

Long sleeves or short sleeves?

Gloves or mittens?

Buttons or zippers?

She even worried about things
she didn't quite understand—
like tennis elbow, and hangnails,
and whether she might need deodorant.

Meanwhile, she
tried to act natural . . .

and *fit* in.

Sometimes Henny
followed Mr. Farmer
around.

He was always very busy.

One day, while he was gathering eggs, one fell.

Henny's arms shot up, and she caught it!

For the rest of the day,

Henny gave Mr. Farmer a hand.

Soon Henny began to imagine all the other things she could do.

She could point.

She could make a point.

She could twiddle her thumbs.

She could cross her arms.

She could pick up little bugs to eat
instead of pecking at them.

She could plug her ears.

She could brush her teeth.

She could comb her comb.

She could carry a purse.

She could carry her purse and hold an umbrella.

She could carry her purse, hold her umbrella,
and hail a taxi in the rain!

She could balance while ice-skating.

She could join the circus.

And maybe,

just maybe . . .

She could fly!